OPOSSUM AND
THE GREAT FIREMAKER

To Sam, Jenna and Katie,
and to the Wednesday night group,
most of all Karen and Carol,
thanks.

Library of Congress Cataloging-in-Publication Data

Mike, Jan M., (date)
    Opossum and the great firemaker: a Mexican legend / written and
adapted by Jan M. Mike; illustrated by Charles Reasoner.
        p.   cm.—(Legends of the world)
    Summary: Relates the traditional Cora Indian tale in which Opossum
outwits the larger and more powerful Iguana and returns the stolen
fire to the people of the earth.
    ISBN 0-8167-3055-5 (lib. bdg.)   ISBN 0-8167-3056-3 (pbk.)
    1. Cora Indians—Legends.   2. Indians of Mexico—Legends.
3. Opossums—Folklore. [1. Cora Indians—Legends.   2. Indians of
Mexico—Legends.   3. Opossums—Folklore.]   I. Reasoner, Charles,
ill.   II. Title.   III. Series.
F1221.C6M54   1993
398.2′089974—dc20   92-36459

OPOSSUM
AND THE GREAT FIREMAKER

A MEXICAN LEGEND

WRITTEN AND ADAPTED BY JAN M. MIKE ILLUSTRATED BY CHARLES REASONER

TROLL ASSOCIATES

Long ago, a small village stood beside the cliff that separated the land from the sky. In the middle of the village, there lived an opossum in a large mango tree. Opossum slept during the day and climbed about looking for food at night.

Opossum was so small that most of the villagers paid her little heed. Even Iguana, the lizard who lived beneath the mango tree, paid no attention to her at all.

Iguana was the Great Firemaker. Tall as any human, he was puffed full of pride. Only he knew how to call out fire from sticks. And when rain washed the fire away, only he could make it blaze again.

One night, as Opossum woke, she heard Iguana complaining to his wife. "It is I who should rule the village," he said, "for I am the Great Firemaker."

"But my husband, there is more to the village than just your fire," said his wife.

"More than my fire!" Iguana shouted. "We shall see."

Late that night, as Opossum hung from a tree branch nibbling a sweet mango, Iguana crept out to the center of the village. He knelt down and swept the village fire into a hollow gourd that he fastened around his waist. Then he ran to the cliff and climbed up, up, up toward the sky.

"Are you coming back soon, Iguana?" called Opossum. Iguana did not answer.

When the morning sun touched the village, Opossum licked the sweet juice from her hands, climbed to her favorite branch, and hung by her tail. She was drifting off to sleep when she heard a young boy shout, "The fire is gone!"

People gathered beneath the mango tree, seeking Iguana and begging him to call out a new fire from sticks. But the Great Firemaker did not answer.

Opossum swung up to sit on the branch, then scampered to the ground. "I know where Iguana is," she said. But, in all the confusion, no one noticed her.

She looked around, spying only ankles and knees, dirt and grass. A large man almost stepped on her. She jumped out of the way. "I saw Iguana leave last night," said little Opossum. But, again, no one listened.

"Iguana has left," his wife said to the crowd.

When the villagers heard this, there was silence. Opossum saw her chance. "Iguana stole the fire. I saw him carry it in a hollow gourd, up, up, up to the sky," she yelled.

This time, everyone heard Opossum. Cries of anger and fear rang out. "We cannot cook our food! Without fire, we will freeze."

"Fire is gone," a young boy shouted, "and no one can bring it back."

"No," a woman answered. "It's only Opossum telling stories. She always gets things mixed up."

Raven flew overhead and perched next to Opossum. He called to the people, "Opossum may be right." Opossum nodded vigorously in agreement. "I have strong wings and sharp eyes. I will fly up to the sky and look for Iguana."

Spreading his black wings, Raven took to the air. Soon he was no more than a speck in the sky.

Beneath the mango tree, the villagers waited. A few stared at Opossum and whispered. She closed her eyes and pretended to be invisible.

"Raven returns!" a sharp-eyed toucan called. Opossum's eyes snapped open.

Raven circled down, his great wings flapping. "I flew till my wings nearly fell from my back," he gasped. "Opossum was right. I saw fire in the sky. Iguana has gone there and taken the fire with him."

"We must send Toucan, Macaw, and Quetzal up to the sky!" the people shouted.

Raven raised one wing for silence.
"No bird can fly that high," he said finally.
"We must find another animal.
One who is quick and clever. One
who can climb."

The crowd grew still. Everyone looked at Opossum. Opossum looked up at the cliff. She was a good climber, but it was a very high cliff, higher than the clouds.

"Will you help us, Opossum?" the people asked. "Will you climb the cliff and bring us fire?"

"No," said Opossum. "You have always ignored me. Why should I help you now?"

"We need you, Opossum," Raven answered softly.

Opossum did not reply. Slowly, the people began to walk away, shivering in the cold wind. Opossum touched her soft white coat. How thick and warm it was!

Opossum swung herself up to sit on the branch. "I will try," she called out. "Wait at the bottom of the cliff. If I can get fire, I will throw it down to you."

Opossum darted to the cliff and grabbed hold of a tiny crevice. Searching for cracks, she began to climb. As she moved higher, the air grew cold. Black rocks cut her hands and feet. Every inch forward was challenged by the rising wind. Above the highest trees, through soft, wet clouds, she climbed. Her arms grew tired. Her small hands ached.

FINALLY, SHE REACHED the top. She smelled wood smoke and looked about. A fire blazed nearby. Before the fire sat Iguana.

Opossum combed her fur with her hands. Then, she spoke. "I have come to visit you, Iguana. May I warm myself by your fire?" she asked.

"No! You will try to steal my fire," Iguana answered.

"You are great and wise, Iguana. Surely, you can guard your fire from someone as small and weak as I."

Iguana raised his crest, preening at Opossum's flattery. "I will tell you stories of my glorious youth," he said.

Opossum sat and pretended to listen as she looked in the fire. A burning stick caught her eye. She raised her hands to touch it. Iguana stopped speaking and glared.

"Speak on, Iguana. I only warm my hands at your lovely fire."

Iguana frowned until she lowered her hands.

Stars wheeled about the sky in their slow dance. Iguana spoke, Opossum stared into the fire. She moved her feet, touching a blazing branch with her toes. Iguana stopped speaking and glared.

"Speak on. I only warm my feet at your lovely fire."

Iguana frowned until she tucked in her feet.

The moon rose, joining the dance of the stars. Iguana spoke, Opossum pretended to listen. She snaked her long white tail out, twisting it around a burning branch.

"You are stealing my fire!" Iguana shouted.

"No! I am raking the coals to make a warmer blaze."

Opossum smelled scorched fur. Soon her tail would begin to sting. Would Iguana never look away? "You look tired, Great Iguana."

"Yes, the warmth
of the fire makes me
sleepy," Iguana admitted.
Iguana stretched. For
the first time, he took
his eyes away from
Opossum.

That was what Opossum had been waiting for. She jumped up and ran.

"*Now* I am taking your fire!" she shouted.

Iguana yelled and raced after Opossum. She carried the burning branch like a torch wrapped in her tail. She ran as quickly as she could, but Iguana followed.

At the edge of the cliff, Opossum flung the flaming branch into the air. Like a shooting star it flew across the sky, down to the land.

"Thief!" Iguana shouted from behind, striking Opossum with a heavy stick.

Opossum curled into a ball, frightened. She had to think quickly. She closed her eyes and lay still as death.

Iguana poked her with his stick. She did not move.

"Are you dead?" he asked Opossum. She did not speak.

Iguana poked her once more. Opossum tumbled over the edge of the cliff and down through the air. Cold wind whistled in her ears and tugged at her fur as she fell.

From below, the people saw her falling.

"We must save Opossum, or she will die!" Raven shouted.

He flew up, beneath Opossum, using his broad wings to break her fall. The people caught her in a blanket. They wrapped her up and brought her to the new fire.

Opossum lay still and silent.

"She is dead," the people cried. "Brave Opossum is dead!"

"No, I am not!" Opossum opened her eyes and sat up. "I am not dead, not even the littlest bit!"

The people were happy. They lifted brave Opossum, carrying her three times around the village while the birds sang their sweetest songs.

Iguana, watching from the cliff, knew he had been fooled. He shook his stick and stamped his feet. As he did so, the ground gave way and he fell, tumbling against the cliffs. Each time Iguana struck the cliff, he grew smaller, until he was no larger than any lizard. When at last he reached the ground, he scuttled away and hid.

Time passed, and people learned to call out fire from sticks. Birds and animals moved off, each to their own place in the forest.

As for Opossum, she still bears the marks of the fire on her smoky gray body and black, hairless tail. If she sees you, she will no doubt fall to the ground, pretending to be dead. It is a trick that has served her well for a long time.

The Sierra Madre, Spanish for "Mother Range," is made up of three mountain ranges that extend along much of coastal Mexico. The western Sierra Madres are home to the Cora Indians, from whom this tale is retold. The Cora Indians are a Náhuatl-Aztec tribe, which means that their language shows their probable ancestors were the mighty Aztecs.

Hundreds of years ago, the Aztecs ruled over a great empire that included much of central and southern Mexico. They built large cities and public schools.

The Aztec system of writing was too basic to record their legends and poetry. So, children had to commit the stories to memory in order to preserve them. In the 1500s, when the Spanish taught people how to write using the alphabet, many of the stories, songs, and poems were written down. Others were lost.

Opossum and the Great Firemaker is an example of a trickster tale. It shows the value placed on cleverness by the tribes of southern Mexico. In the story, Opossum outsmarts a creature who is larger and more powerful than herself. The trickster can be found in many cultures. Ananse the Spider in Africa, Coyote in the American Southwest, and Raven in the Pacific Northwest are just a few examples of these clever heroes.

Mexican iguana